The Three Bears
and a Very Hungry Golidlocks

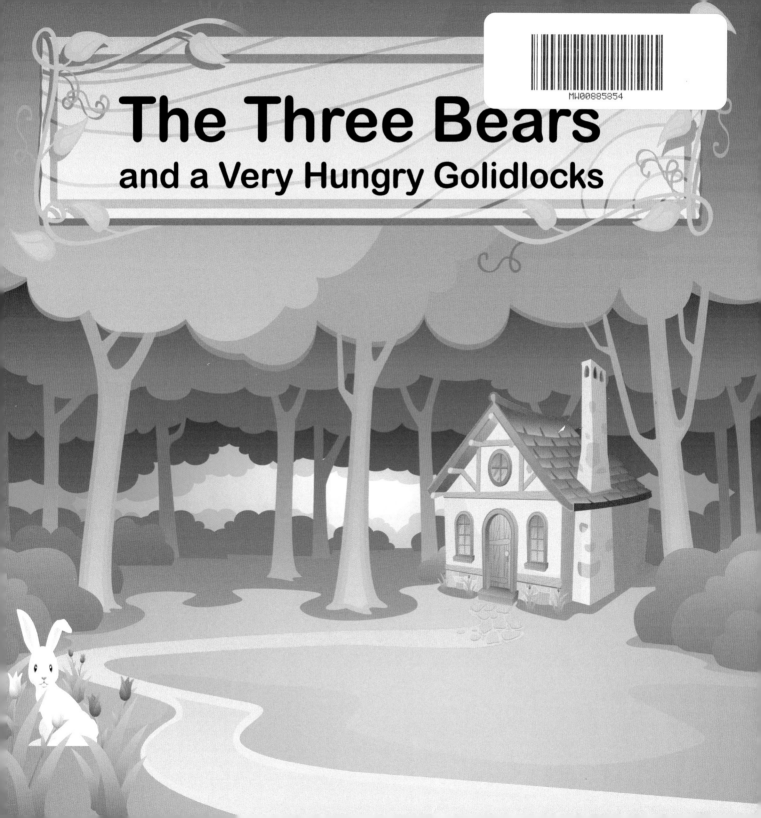

Published by Kemet Toy & Game Co.
For information on bulk purchases or to book the author please contact
www.KemetToys.com or email: support@kemettoys.com Phone: 347-855-4235

Stay in touch via social media: @kemetkids (Instagram, Facebook, Youtube, Twitter)

Please help more readers discover this book by leaving a 5-STAR Review.

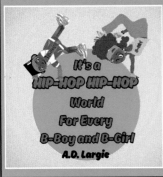   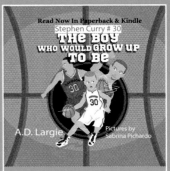

Once upon a time there were three bears that lived in the forest.

There was Papa Bear, Mama Bear and Baby Bear.

It was dinner time in the Bear Family house so Mama Bear called out... "Papa Bear and Baby Bear come to dinner!"

Papa Bear and Baby Bear rush to sit down at the dinner table.

Mama Bear shared the food and they all sat down ready to eat.

Baby Bear tasted his food but as soon as it touched his mouth he said. "Ouch! Ouch! My food is too hot."

So Papa Bear, Mama Bear and Baby Bear dressed up, put on their shoes and they all went out to the park.

At the park Baby Bear was having so much fun, climbing, jumping, running and playing.

Meanwhile, back at the Bear Family home there was another bear. This bear's name was Hungry Bear.

Hungry Bear was very, very hungry. She was looking through the window at all that delicious food on the table and she really wanted to eat it.

She tried to get in through the front door but it was locked so she had to climb through the window.

As soon as Hungry Bear climbed inside, she sat down in Baby Bear's chair.

Hungry Bear tasted Baby Bear's food and said "umm yummy" then ate all of Baby Bear's food.

Then she sat down in Papa Bear's chair and ate all of Papa Bear's food. Soon after she sat down in Mama Bear's chair and and ate all of Mama Bear's food too.

After eating sooo much food, Hungry Bear felt very, very sleepy.

So she found Baby Bear's bed and fell asleep like this. "ZZZ-Zzzz-ZZzzz-hngGG-ggh-Ppbhww- zZZzzzZZ . . ."

While Hungry Bear was sleeping someone was opening the front door. Do you know who it is?

It was Mama Bear, Papa Bear and Baby Bear returning home from the park and they were all very, very hungry.

So, Papa Bear, Mama Bear and Baby Bear quickly took off their shoes changed their clothes and sat down at the dinner table.

Baby Bear looked at his plate and started crying. "Waa...Waah! Somebody ate all my food! Waa...Waah!"

Then Papa Bear said, "somebody ate all my food too."

Mama Bear said "I wonder who ate all of our food?" Then they all heard a sound.

ZZZ-Zzzz-ZZzzz-hngGGggh-Ppbhww-zZZzzzZZ . . .

What is that sound?

It was the sound of Hungry Bear snoring.

Baby Bear jumped up and dashed off to find out where the sound was coming from. Then he screamed out... "Papa Bear ! Mama Bear! come quick."

"Someone is sleepying in my bed!" With all the screaming, Hungry Bear woke up like.. "uh...uh what's going on?"
Baby Bear pointed at Hungry Bear and asked "did you eat all my food?"

Hungry Bear said, "Yes. I ate all your food because I was very, very hungry."

Then Papa Bear picked up Hungry Bear by the back of her shirt, ready to throw her out the front door.

When Mama Bear screamed out...

"STOP!"

"Where is your Mama and your Daddy?"

Hungry Bear said...

"I don't have Mama and Daddy."

Then, Mama Bear said "put her down right now."

So Papa Bear put down Hungry Bear then Mama Bear asked, "are you still very, very hungry?"

Hungry Bear said, "Yes, I'm still very, very hungry."

Mama Bear said, "then go sit down at the dinner table." She turned to Baby Bear and said, "you go sit down at the table." She turned to Papa Bear and said, "you go sit down at the table too."

Then Mama brought more food and everybody ate until their stomach was very, very full.

Then Mama Bear said, "Hungry Bear, since you don't have a Mommy and Daddy we will be your new Mommy and Daddy." And everyone lived happily ever after and none of them was ever hungry again.

THE END

Made in the USA
Columbia, SC
21 November 2020